A KNYGHT THER WAS

A KNYGHT THER WAS

Robert F. Young

A Knyght ther was, and that a worthy man, That fro the tyme that he first bigan to ryden out, he loved chivalrye, trouthe and honour, fredom and curteisye
—THE CANTERBURY TALES

I

Mallory, who among other things was a time-thief, re-materialized the time-space boat *Yore* in the eastern section of a secluded valley in ancient Britain and typed CASTLE, EARLY SIXTH-CENTURY on the lumillusion panel. Then he stepped over to the control-room telewindow and studied the three-dimensional screen. The hour was 8:00 p.m.; the season, summer; the Year 542 A.D.

Darkness was on hand, but there was a full moon rising and he could see trees not far away—oaks and beeches, mostly. Roving the eye of the camera, he saw more trees of the same species. The "castle of Yore" was safely ensconced in a forest. Satisfied, he turned away.

If his calculations were correct, the castle of Carbonek stood in the next valley to the south, and on a silver table in a chamber of the castle stood the object of his quest.

If his calculations were correct.

Mallory was not one to keep himself in suspense. Stepping into the supply room, he stripped down to his undergarments and proceeded to get into the custom-built suit of armor which he had purchased expressly for the operation. Fortunately, while duplication of early sixth-century design had been mandatory, there had been no need to duplicate early sixth-century materials, and sollerets, spurs, greaves, cuisses, breastplate, pauldrons, gorget, arm-coverings, gauntlets, helmet, and chain-mail vest had all been fashioned of light-weight alloys that lent ten times as much protection at ten times less poundage. The helmet was his particular pride and joy: in keeping with the period-piece after which it had been patterned, it looked like an upside-down metal wastepaper basket, but the one-way transparency of the special alloy that had gone into its construction gave him unrestricted vision, while two inbuilt audio-amplifiers performed a corresponding service for his hearing.

The outer surface of each piece had been burnished to a high degree, and he found himself a dazzling sight indeed when he looked into the supply-room mirror. This effect was enhanced no end when he buckled on his chrome-plated scabbard and red-hilted sword and hung his snow-white shield around his neck. His polished spear, when he stood it beside him, was almost anticlimactic. It shouldn't have been. It was a good three and one-half inches in diameter at the base, and it was as tall as a young flagpole.

As he stood there looking at his reflection, the red cross in the center of the shield took on the hue of freshly-shed blood. The period-piece expert who had designed the shield had insisted on the illusion, saying that it made for greater authenticity, and Mallory hadn't argued with him. He was glad now that he hadn't. Raising the visor of his helmet, he winked at himself and said, "I hereby christen ye 'Sir Galahad'."

Next, he bethought himself of his steed. Armor clanking, he left the supply room and walked down the short passage to the rec-hall. The rec-hall occupied the entire forward section of the TSB and had been designed solely for the benefit of the time-tourists whom Mallory regularly conducted on past-tours as a cover-up for the illegal activities which he pursued in between trips. In the present instance, however, the hall went quite well with the *Yore's* lumillusioned exterior, possessing, with its gallery-like mezzanine, its long snack table, and its imitation flagstone flooring, an early sixth-century aspect of its own—an aspect marred only slightly by the "anachronistic" telewindows inset at regular intervals along the walls.

Mallory's steed stood in a stall-like enclosure that was formed by the tourist-bar and one of the walls, and it was a splendid "beast" indeed—as splendid a one as the twenty-second century robotics industry was capable of creating. Originally, Mallory had planned on bringing a real horse with him, but as this would have necessitated his having to learn how to ride, he had decided against it. The decision had been a wise one: "Easy Money" looked more like a horse than most real horses did, could travel twice as fast, and was as easy to ride and to maneuver as a golp jetney. It was light-brown in color with a white diamond on its forehead, it was equipped with a secret croup-compartment and an inbuilt saddle, and its fetlock-length trappings were made of genuine synthisilk threaded with gold. It wore no armor—it did not need to: weapons manufactured during the Age of Chivalry could no more penetrate its "hide" than a tooth pick could.

Come on, Easy Money, Mallory encephalopathed. *You and I have a little job to do.*

The rohorse emitted several realistic whinnies, backed out of its "stall," trotted smartly over to his side, and nuzzled his right pauldron. Mallory mounted—not gracefully, it is true, but at least without the aid of the winch he would have needed if his armor had been manufactured in the sixth century—and inserted the red pommel of his spear in the stirrup socket. Then, activating the *Yore's* lock, he rode across the imaginary drawbridge that spanned the mirage-moat, and set forth into the forest. As the "portcullis" closed behind him, symbolically bringing phase one of Operation Sangraal to a close, he thought of Jason Perfidion.

*

Standing in front of the floor-to-ceiling, wall-to-wall fireplace in the big balconied room, Perfidion said, "Mallory, you're wasting your time. Worse, you're wasting mine."

The room climaxed a vertical series of slightly less sumptuous chambers known collectively as the Perfidion Tower, and the Perfidion Tower stood with a score of balconied brothers on a blacktop island in the exact center of Kansas' largest golp course. A short distance from the fraternal gathering stood yet another tower—the false tower into which Mallory had lumillusioned his TSB upon his arrival. On the Golp Terrace, as the blacktop island was called, everyone and everything conformed—or else.

The room itself was known to time-thieves as "Perfidion's Lair." And yet there was nothing about Jason Perfidion—nothing physical, that is—that suggested the predator. He was Mallory's age—thirty-three—tall, dark of hair, and strikingly handsome. He looked like—and was—a highly successful businessman with a triplex on Get-Rich-Quick Street, and he gave the impression that he was as honest as the day was long. Just the same, the predator was there, and if you were alert enough you could sometimes glimpse it peering out through the smoky windowpanes of his eyes.

It wasn't peering out now, though. It was sleeping. However, it was due to wake up any second. "Then you're not interested in fencing the Holy Grail?" Mallory asked.

Annoyance intensified the slight swarthiness of Perfidion's cheeks. "Mallory, you know as well as I do that the Grail never really existed, that it was nothing more than the mead-inspired daydream of a bunch of quixotic knights. So go and get your hair cut and forget about it."

"But suppose it *did* exist," Mallory insisted. "Suppose, tomorrow afternoon at this time, I were to come in here and set it down on this desk here? How much could you get for it?"

Perfidion laughed. "How much *couldn't* I get for it! Why, without even stopping to think I can name you a dozen collectors who'd give their right arm for it."

"I'm not interested in right arms," Mallory said. "I'm interested in dollars. How many Kennedees could you get for it?"

"A megamillion—maybe more. More than enough, certainly, to permit you to retire from time-lifting and to take up residence on Get-Rich-Quick Street. But it doesn't exist, and it never did, so get out of here, Mallory, and stop squandering my valuable time."

Mallory withdrew a small stereophoto from his breast pocket and tossed it on the desk. "Have a look at that first—then I'll go," he said.

Perfidion picked up the photo. "An ordinary enough yellow bowl," he began, and stopped. Suddenly he gasped, and jabbed one of the many buttons that patterned his desktop. Seconds later, a svelte blonde whom Mallory had never seen before stepped out of the lift tube. Like most general-purpose secretaries, she wore a maximum of makeup and a minimum of clothing, and moved in an aura of efficiency and sex. "Get me my photo-projector, Miss Tyler," Perfidion said.

When she returned with it, he set it on his desk and inserted the stereophoto. Instantly, a huge cube materialized in the center of the room. Inside the cube there was a realistic image of a resplendent silver table, and upon the image of the table stood an equally realistic image of a resplendent golden bowl. Perfidion gasped again.

"Unusual workmanship, wouldn't you say?" Mallory said.

Perfidion turned toward the blonde. "You may go, Miss Tyler."

She was staring at the contents of the cube and apparently did not hear him. "I said," he repeated, "that you may go, Miss Tyler."

8

"Oh. Yes . . . yes sir."

*

When the lift-tube door closed behind her, Perfidion turned to Mallory. For a fraction of a second the predator was visible behind the smoky windowpanes of his eyes; then, quickly, it ducked out of sight. "Where was this taken, Tom?"

"It's a distance-shot," Mallory said. "I took it through one of the windows of the church Joseph of Arimathea built in Glastonbury."

"But how did you know—"

"That it was there? Because it *had* to be there. Some time ago, while escorting a group of tourists around ancient Britain, I happened to witness Joseph of Arimathea's landing—and happened to catch a glimpse of what he brought with him. I used to think that the Grail was a pipe dream, too, but when I saw it with my own eyes, I knew that it couldn't have been. However, I knew I'd need evidence to convince you, so I jumped back to a later place-time and got a shot of it."

"But why a shot, Tom? Why didn't you lift it then and there?"

"You concede that it is the Grail then?"

"Of course it's the Grail—there's not the slightest question about it. Why didn't you lift it?"

"Well, for one thing, I wanted to make sure that lifting it would be worth my while, and for another, Glastonbury wasn't the logical place-time from which to lift it, because, assuming that the rest of the legend is also true, it was seen after that place-time. No time-thief ever bucked destiny yet and came out the winner, Jason; I play my percentages."

"I know you do, Tom. You're one of the best time-lift men in the business, and the Past Police would be the first to admit it . . . . I daresay you've already pinpointed the key place-time?"

Mallory grinned, showing his white teeth. "I certainly have, but if you think I'm going to divulge it, you're sadly mistaken, Jason. And stop looking at my hair—it won't tell you anything beyond the fact that I've been using Hairhaste. Shoulder-length hair was the rage in more eras than one."

Perfidion smiled warmly, and clapped Mallory on the back. "I'm not trying to ferret out your secret, Tom. I know better than that. Lifting is your line, fencing mine. You bring me the Grail, I'll sell it, take my cut, and everything will be fine. You know me, Tom."

"I sure do," Mallory said, taking the stereophoto out of the projector and returning it to his breast pocket.

Perfidion snapped his fingers. "A happy thought just occurred to me! I've got a golp date with Rowley of Puriproducts, so why don't you join us, Tom? You play a pretty good game, as I recall."

Mollified, Mallory said, "I'll have to borrow a set of your jetsticks."

"I'll get them for you on the way down. Come on, Tom."

Mallory accompanied him across the room. "Keep mum about this to Rowley now," Perfidion said confidentially. "He's a potential customer, but we don't want to let the cat out of the bag yet, do we? Or should I say 'the Grail'." He took time out to grin at his little joke, then, "By the way, Tom, I take it you're all set as regards costume, equipment and the like."

"I've got the sweetest little suit of armor you ever laid eyes on," Mallory said.

"Fine—no need for me to offer any advice in that respect then." Perfidion opened the lift door. "After you, Tom."

They plummeted down the tube together.

*

It had been a good game of golp—from Mallory's standpoint, anyway. He had trounced Rowley roundly, and he would have inflicted similar ignominy upon Perfidion had not the latter been called away in the middle of the game and been unable to return till it was nearly over. Oh well, Mallory thought, encephalo-guiding his rohorse through the ancient forest, there'll be other chances. Aloud, he said, "Step lively now, Easy Money, and let's get this caper over with so we can return to civilization and start feeling what it's like to be rich."

In response to the encephalo-waves that had accompanied his words, Easy Money increased its pace, the infra-red rays of its eye units illumining its way. In places, light from the rising moon seeped through the foliage, but otherwise darkness was the rule. The air was cool and damp—the sea was not far distant—and the sound of frogs and insects was omnipresent and now and then there was the rustling sound of some small and fleeing forest creature.

10

Presently the ground began to rise, and not long afterward the trees thinned out temporarily and rohorse and rider emerged on the moonlit crest of the ridge that separated the two valleys. In the distance Mallory made out the moon-gilt towers and turrets of a large castle, and knew it to be Carbonek beyond a doubt. He sighed with relief. He was all set now—provided his masquerade went over. Conversely, if it didn't go over he was finished: his sword and his spear were his only weapons, and his shield and his armor, his only protection. True, each article was superior in quality and durability to its corresponding article in the Age of Chivalry, but otherwise none of them was anything more than what it seemed. Mallory might be a time-thief; but within the framework of his profession he believed in playing fair.

In response to his encephalopathed directions, Easy Money picked its way down the slope of the ridge and re-entered the forest. Not long afterward it stepped onto what was euphemistically referred to in that day and age as a "highway" but which in reality was little more than a wide, hoof-trampled lane. As Mallory's entire plan of action was based on boldness, he spurned the shadows of the bordering oaks and beeches and encephalopathed the rohorse to keep to the center of the lane. He met no one, however, despite the earliness of the hour, nor had he really expected to. It was highly improbable that any freemen would be abroad after dark, and as for the knight-errants who happened to be in the neighborhood, it was highly improbable that any of them would be abroad after dark either.

He grinned. To read *Le Morte d'Arthur*, you'd think that the chivalry boys had been in business twenty-four hours a day, slaying ogres, rescuing fair damosels, and searching for the Sangraal; but not if you read between the lines. Mallory had read "Arthur" only cursorily, but he had had a hunch all along that in the majority of cases the quest for the Sangraal had served as an out, and that the knights of the Table Round had spent more time wenching and wassailing than they had conducting their so-called dedicated search, and the hunch had played an important role in the shaping of his strategy.

The highway turned this way and that, never pursuing a straight course unless such a logical procedure was unavoidable. Once, he thought he heard hoofbeats up ahead, but he met no one, and not long afterward he saw the pale pile of Carbonek looming above the trees to his left, and encephalo-

11

guided Easy Money into the lane that led to the entrance. There was no moat, but the portcullis was an imposing one. Flanking it on either side was a huge stone lion, and framing it were flaming torches in regularly-spaced niches. Warders in hauberk and helmet looked down from the lofty wall, their halberds gleaming in the dancing torchlight. Mallory swallowed: the moment of truth had arrived.

He halted Easy Money and canted his white shield so that the red cross in its center would be visible from above. Then he marshalled his smattering of Old English. "I hight Sir Galahad of the Table Round," he called out in as bold a voice as he could muster. "I would rest my eyes upon the Sangraal."

*

Instantly, confusion reigned upon the wall as the warders vied with one another for the privilege of operating the cumbersome windlass that raised and lowered the portcullis, and presently, to the accompaniment of a chorus of creaks and groans and scrapings, the ponderous iron grating began to rise. Mallory forced himself to wait until it had risen to a height befitting a knight of Sir Galahad's caliber, then he rode through the gateway and into the courtyard, congratulating himself on the effectiveness of his impersonation.

"Ye will come unto the chamber of the Sangraal sixty paces down the corridor to thy left eftsoon ye enter the chief fortress, sir knight," one of the warders called down. "An ye had arrived a little while afore, ye had encountered Sir Launcelot du Lake, the which did come unto the fortress and enter in, wherefrom he came out anon and departed."

Mallory would have wiped his forehead if his forehead had been accessible and if his hands had not been encased in metal gloves. Fooling the warders was one thing, but passing himself off as Sir Galahad to the man who was Sir Galahad's father would have been quite another. He had learned from the pages of his near-namesake's "Arthur" that Sir Launcelot had visited Carbonek before Sir Galahad had, but the pages had not revealed whether the time-lapse had involved minutes, hours, or years, and for that matter, Mallory wasn't altogether certain whether the second visit they described had been the real Sir Galahad's, which meant failure, or a romanticized version of his own, which meant success. His near-namesake was murky at best, and reading him you were never sure where anybody was, or when any given event was taking place.

The courtyard was empty, and after crossing it, Mallory dismounted, encephalopathed Easy Money to stay put, and climbed the series of stone steps that led to the castle proper. Entering the building unchallenged, he found himself at the junction of three corridors. The main one stretched straight ahead and debouched into a large hall. The other two led off at right angles, one to the left and one to the right. Boisterous laughter emanated from the hall, and he could see knights and other nobles sitting at a long banquet table. Scattered among them were gentlewomen in rich silks, and hovering behind them were servants bearing large demijohns. He grinned. Just as he had figured—King Pelles was throwing a whingding.

Quickly, Mallory turned down the left-hand corridor and started along it, counting his footsteps. Rushes rustled beneath his feet, and the flickering light of wall-torches gave him a series of grotesque shadows. He saw no one: all the servants were in the banquet hall, pouring wine and mead. He laughed aloud.

Forty-eight paces sufficed to see him to the chamber door. It was a perfectly ordinary door. Opening it, he thought at first that the room beyond was ordinary, too. Then he saw the burning candles arranged along the walls, and beneath them, standing in the center of the floor, the table of silver. The table of the Sangraal . . . .

There was no Sangraal on the table, however. There was no Sangraal in the room, for that matter. There was a girl, though. She was huddled forlornly in a corner, and she was crying.

II

Mallory laid his spear aside, strode across the room, and raised the girl to her feet. "The Sangraal," he said, forgetting in his agitation the few odds and ends of Old English he had memorized. "Where is it!"

She raised startled eyes that were as round, and almost as large, as plums. Her face was round, too, and faintly childlike. Her hair was dark-brown, and done up in a strange and indeterminate coiffeur that was as charming as it was disconcerting. Her ankle-length dress was white, and there was a bow on the bodice that matched the plum-blueness of her eyes. A few cosmetics, properly applied, would have turned her into an attractive woman, and even without them, she rated a second look.

She stared at him for some time, then, "Surely ye be an advision, sir," she said. "I . . . I know ye not."

Mallory swung his shield around so that she could see the red cross. "Now do you know me?"

She gasped, and her eyes grew even rounder. "Sir . . . Sir Galahad! Oh, fair knight, wherefore did ye not say?"

Mallory ignored the question. "The Sangraal," he repeated. "Where is it?"

Her tears had ceased temporarily; now they began again. "Oh, fair sir!" she cried, "ye see tofore you, a damosel at mischief, the which was given guardianship of the Holy Vessel at her own request, and bewrayed her trust, a damosel—"

"Never mind all that," Mallory said. "Where's the Sangraal?"

"I wot not, fair sir."

"But you must know if you were guarding it!"

"I wot not whither it was taken."

"But you must wot who took it."

"Wot I well, fair knight. Sir Launcelot, the which is thy father, bare it from the chamber."

Mallory was stunned. "But that's impossible! My fa—Sir Launcelot wouldn't steal the Sangraal!"

"Well I wot, fair sir; yet steal it he did. Came he unto the chamber and saith, I hight Sir Launcelot du Lake of the Table Round, whereat I did see his

14

armor to be none other; so then took he the Vessel covered with the red samite and bare it with him from the chamber, whereat I—"

"How long ago?"

"But a little while afore eight of the clock. Sithen I have wept. I know now no good knight, nor no good man. And I know from thy holy shield and from they good name that thou art a good knight, and I beseech ye therefore to help me, for ye be a shining knight indeed, wherefore ye ought not to fail no damosel which is in distress, and she besought you of help."

Mallory only half heard her. Sir Launcelot was too much with him. It was inconceivable that a knight of such noble principles would even consider touching the Sangraal, to say nothing of making off with it. Maybe, though, his principles hadn't been quite as noble as they had been made out to be. He had been Queen Guinevere's paramour, hadn't he? He had lain with the fair Elaine, hadn't he? When you came right down to it, he could very well have been a scoundrel at heart all along—a scoundrel whose true nature had been toned down by writers like Malory and poets like Tennyson. All of which, while it strongly suggested that he was capable of stealing the Sangraal, threw not the slightest light on his reason for having done so. Mallory was right back where he had started from.

He turned to the girl. "You said something about needing my help. What do you want me to do?"

Instantly, her tears stopped and she clasped her hands together and looked at him with worshipful eyes. "Oh, fair sir, ye be most kind indeed! Well I wot from thy shining armor that ye—"

"Knock it off," Mallory said.

"Knock it off? I wot not what—"

"Never mind. Just tell me what you want me to do."

"Ye must bear me from the castle, fair sir, or the king learns I have bewrayed my trust and wreaks his wrath upon me. And then ye must help me regain the Holy Cup and return it to this chamber."

"We'll worry about getting the Cup back after we're beyond the walls," Mallory said, starting for the door. "Come on—they're all in the banquet hall and as drunk as lords—they won't even see us go by."

She hung back. "But the warders, fair sir—they be not enchafed. And King Pelles, by my own wish, did forbid them to pass me."

Mallory stared at her. "By your own wish! Well of all the crazy—" Abruptly he dropped the subject. "All right then—how *do* we get out of here?"

"There lieth beneath the fortress and the forest a parlous passage wherein dwells the fiend, the which I have much discomfit of. But with ye aside me, fair knight, there is naught to fear."

Mallory had read enough Malory to be able to take sixth-century fiends in his stride. "I'll have to take my horse along," he said. "Is there room for it to pass?"

"Yea, fair sir. The tale saith that aforetime many knights did ride out beneath the fortress and the forest and did smite the Saxons, Saracens, and Pagans, the which did compass the castle about, from behind, whereupon the battle was won."

Mallory stepped outside the chamber, the girl just behind him, and encephalopathed the necessary directions. After a moment, Easy Money came trotting down the corridor to his side. The girl gasped, and, to his astonishment, threw her arms around the rohorse's neck. "He is a noble steed indeed, fair sir," she said; "and worthy of a knight fitting to sit in the Siege Perilous." Presently she stepped back, frowning. "He . . . he is most cold, fair sir."

"All horses of that breed are," Mallory explained. "Incidentally, his name is 'Easy Money'."

"La! such a strange name."

"Not so strange." Mallory raised his visor, making a mental note to see to it that any and all suits of armor he might buy in the future were air-conditioned. He got his spear. "Let's be on our way, shall we?"

"Ye . . . ye have blue eyes, fair sir."

"Never mind the color of my eyes—let's get out of here."

She seemed to make up her mind about something. "An ye will follow me, sir knight," she said, and started down the corridor.

*

A ramp, the entrance of which was camouflaged by a rotating section of the inner castle wall, gave access to the subterranean passage. The passage itself, in the flickering light of the torch that the girl had brought along, appeared at first to be nothing more than a natural cave enlarged through the centuries by the stream that still flowed down its center. Presently, however, Mallory saw that in certain places the stone walls had been cut back in such a way that the space on either side of the stream never narrowed to a width of less than four feet. He saw other evidence of human handiwork too—dungeons. They were little more than shallow caves now, though, their iron gratings having rusted and fallen away.

After proceeding half a hundred yards, he paused. "I don't know what we're walking for when we've got a perfectly good horse at our disposal," he told the girl. "Come on, I'll help you into the saddle and I'll jump on behind."

She shook her head. "No, fair knight, it is not fitting for a gentlewoman to ride tofore her champion. Ye will mount, and I will ride behind."

"Suit yourself," Mallory said. He climbed into the saddle with a clank and a clatter, and helped her up on Easy Money's croup. "By the way, you never did tell me your name."

"I hight the damosel Rowena."

"Pleased to meet you," Mallory said. *Giddy-ap, Easy Money,* he encephalopathed.

They rode in silence for a little while, the light from Rowena's torch dancing acappella rigadoons on bare walls and dripping ceilings, Easy Money's hoofbeats hardly audible above the purling of the stream. Presently Rowena said, "It were best that ye drew out thy sword, fair sir, for anon the fiend will beset us."

"He hasn't beset us yet," Mallory pointed out.

"La! fair sir, he will."

He saw no harm in humoring her, and did as she had suggested. "You mentioned something a while back about having been given guardianship of the Sangraal at your own request," he said. "How did that come about?"

"List, fair sir, and I will tell ye. But first I must tell ye of Sir Bors de Ganis, of which Sir Lionel is brother. It happed one day that Sir Bors did ride into a forest in the Kingdom of Mennes unto the hour of midday, and there befell him a marvelous adventure. So he met at the departing of the two ways two knights that led Lionel, his brother, all naked, bounden upon a strong hackney, and his hands bounden tofore his breast. And every each of them held in his hands thorns wherewith they went beating him so sore that the blood trailed down more than in an hundred places of his body, so that he was all blood tofore and behind, but he said never a word; as he which was great of heart he suffered all that ever they did to him as though he had felt none anguish.

"Anon Sir Bors dressed him to rescue him that was his brother; and so he looked upon the other side of him, and saw a knight which brought a fair gentlewoman, and would have set her in the thickest place of the forest for to have been the more surer out of the way from them that sought him. And she which was nothing assured cried with a high voice: 'Saint Mary succor your maid.' And anon she espied where Sir Bors came riding. And when she came nigh him she deemed him a knight of the Round Table, whereof she hoped to have some comfort; and then she conjured him: By the faith that he ought unto him in whose service thou art entered in, and for the faith ye owe unto the high order of knighthood, and for the noble King Arthur's sake, that I suppose that made thee knight, that thou help me, and suffer me not to be shamed of this knight. When—"

"Just a minute," Mallory interrupted, thoroughly bewildered and simultaneously afflicted with an irrational sense of *deja vu*. "This gentlewoman you speak of—would she by any chance be you?"

"Wit ye well, fair sir. When—"

"But if she's you, why don't you use the first person singular instead of the third?"

"I wot not what—"

"Why don't you use 'I' instead of 'she' when you refer to yourself directly?"

"It would not be fitting, fair knight. When Bors heard her say thus he had so much sorrow there he nyst not what to do. For if I let my brother be in adventure he must be slain, and that would I not for all the earth. And if I help not the maid she is shamed for ever, and also she shall lose her virginity the which she shall never get again. Then lift he up his eyes and said weeping: Fair sweet Lord, whose liege man I am, keep Lionel, my brother, that these knights slay him not, and for pity of you, and for Mary's sake, I shall succor this maid. Then dressed he him unto the knight the which had the gentlewoman, and then—"

*

"Hist!" Mallory whispered. "I heard something."

For a moment the light flared wildly as though she had nearly dropped the torch. "Wh . . . whence came the sound, fair knight?"

"From the other side of the stream." He peered into the vacillating shadows, but saw nothing but the darker shadows of one of the innumerable man-made caves. The sound he had heard had brought to mind the dull clang that metal makes when it collides with stone, and it had been so faint as to have been barely audible above the purling of the stream. Thinking back, he was not altogether certain that he had heard it at all. "My imagination's getting the best of me, I guess," he said presently. "There's no one there."

Her warm breath penetrated the crevices of his gorget and fanned the back of his neck. "Ye . . . ye ween not that it could have been the fiend prowling?"

"Of course I ween not! Relax, and finish your story. But get to the point, will you?"

"An . . . an it so please . . . . And then Sir Bors cried: Sir knight, let your hand off that maiden, or ye be but dead. And then he set down the maiden, and was armed at all pieces save he lacked his spear. Then he dressed his shield, and drew out his sword, and Bors smote him so hard that it went through his shield and habergeon on the left shoulder. And through great strength he beat him down to the earth, and at the pulling out of Bors' spear there he swooned. Then came Bors to the maid and said: How seemeth it to you of this knight ye be delivered at this time? Now sir, said she, I pray you lead me there as this knight had me. So shall I do gladly: and took the horse of the wounded knight, and set the gentlewoman upon him, and so brought her as she desired. Sir knight, said she, ye have better sped than ye weened, for an I had lost my maidenhead, five hundred men should have died for it. What knight was he that had you in the forest? By my faith, said she, he is my cousin. So wot I never with what engyn the fiend enchafed him, for yesterday he took me from my father privily; for I nor none of my father's men

19

mistrusted him not, and if he had had my maidenhead he should have died for the sin, and his body shamed and dishonored for ever. Thus as—"

"*Shhh!*"

This time, Mallory was certain that he had heard something. The sound had had much in common with the previous sound, except that it had suggested metal scraping against, rather than colliding with, stone. Directly across the stream was another cave, this one shallow enough to permit the torchlight to penetrate its deeper shadows, and looking into those shadows, he caught a faint gleam of reflected light.

Rowena must have caught it, too, for he heard her gasp behind him. "It were best that I thanked ye now for thy great kindness, fair knight," she said, "for anon we be no longer on live."

"Nonsense!" Mallory said. "If this fiend of yours is anywhere in the vicinity, he's probably more afraid of us than we are of him."

The cave was behind them now. "Per . . . peradventure he hath already had meat," Rowena said hopefully. "The tale saith that and the fiend be filled, he becomes aweary and besets not them the which do pass him by in peace."

"I'll keep my sword handy, just in case he changes his mind," Mallory said. "Meanwhile, get on with your autobiography—only for Pete's sake, cut it short, will you?"

"An it please, fair sir. Thus as the fair gentlewoman stood talking with Sir Bors there came twelve knights seeking after her, and anon she told them all how Bors had delivered her; then they made great joy, and besought him to come to her father, a great lord, and he should be right welcome. Truly, said Bors, that may not be at this time, for I have a great adventure to do in this country. So he commended them unto God and departed. The fair gentlewoman did grieve mickle to see him leave, and she saith, sir knights, noble was the service that brave knight did render unto thy liege's daughter in the saving of her maidenhead the which she could never get again, for that be none other than his own brother the which he fauted. Therefore, noble must be both his king and his cause, wherefore it be befitting that a gentlewoman of thy liege's daughter's nature leave the castle of her father betimes that she may render fitting service to her succor's cause and be worthy of his deed. Thus spake this fair gentlewoman, whereat she did mount upon her palfrey and so departed her from thence and did ride as fast as her palfrey might bear her, whereupon after many days she came to the castle of Carbonek and did seek out King Pelles and did beseech him that she might be made guardian of the Sangraal, whereat he did graciously consent to her request and did consent also that she be made prisoner in the fortress by her own wish. And now she was bewrayed her trust, fair sir, and the table of silver whereon the Sangraal stood stands empty."

*

For some time after she finished talking, Mallory was silent. Was she trying to pull his leg? he wondered. Or were the gentlewomen of her day and age really as high-minded and as feathered-brained as she would have him believe? He decided not to go into the matter for the moment. "Tell me, Rowena," he said, "if the Sangraal is visible only to those who are worthy of it, as I have been led to believe, how are any of those wassailers whooping it up back there in that banquet hall going to know whether it's gone or not?"

"It be ofttimes averred that all cannot see the Holy Cup, as ye say, fair knight. Natheless, all that have come unto the chamber sithen my trust began, they did see it, and Sir Launcelot, the which is much with sin, he did see it—and did take it."

"He's not going to get very far with it, though," Mallory said. And then, "How long is the tunnel anyway?"

"Anon we shall see the stars, fair sir."

She was right, and a few minutes later, after rounding a turn in the passage, they emerged upon the bank of a small river. The subterranean stream that had kept them company emerged, too, and joined its larger sister on the way to the sea. On either hand, cliffs rose up, and the susurrus of waves breaking on sand could be heard in the distance.

Mallory guided Easy Money upstream to where the cliffs dwindled down to thickly forested slopes. It took him but a moment to orientate himself, and presently rohorse and riders were headed in the direction of the highway. "Now," said he, "if you'll tell me where you want to be dropped off, I'll see what I can do about getting the Grail back."

There was a brief silence. Then, "An . . . an ye wish, ye may leave me here."

21

He halted Easy Money, dismounted, and lifted her down to the ground. He looked around, expecting to see a habitation of some sort. He saw nothing but trees. He faced the girl again. "Don't you have any friends or relatives you can stay with?"

An argent shaft of moonlight slanting down through the foliage illumined her face. "There be none nigh, fair sir, nor none nearer than an hundred miles. I shall abide your again coming here in the forest."

Mallory stared at her. She didn't look—or act either, for that matter—as though she knew enough to get in out of the rain. "Abide here in the forest! Why, you wouldn't last a week!"

"But ye will return hither with the Sangraal long afore that, whereupon we two together shall return the Holy Vessel to the chamber and I shall not be made to suffer the severing of my two hands."

He was aghast. "They wouldn't dare cut off your hands!"

"They dare much, fair knight. Know ye naught of the customs of the land?"

He was silent. What in the world was he going to do about her? She would probably wait here for him until she starved to death or, equally as distressing, until she was apprehended. Abruptly he shrugged his shoulders—to the extent that his pauldrons permitted—and remounted the rohorse. Why should it matter to him what became of her? He'd returned to the Age of Chivalry to steal the Sangraal, not to play nursemaid to damosels in distress. "Don't take any wooden nickels now," he said.

Two tiny stars appeared in the pale regions of her eyes and twinkled down her cheeks. "May the good Lord speed ye upon thy quest, fair knight, and may He guard ye well."

"Oh, for Pete's sake!" Mallory said, and reaching down, pulled her up onto Easy Money's croup. "I have a castle not far from here. I'll drop you off, then I'll go after the Sangraal."

Her breath was warm little wind seeping through the crevices of his gorget. "Oh, fair sir, ye be the noblest of all the knights in all the land, and I shall serve thee faithfully for the rest of my days!"

The rohorse whinnied. *Giddy-ap, Easy Money,* Mallory encephalopathed, and they started out.

III

Rowena fell for the *Yore* hook, line, and sinker. Not even the modern interior gave her pause. Those objects which happened to be beyond her ken—and there were many of them—she interpreted as "appointments befitting a noble knight," and as for the rooms themselves, she merely identified them with the rooms out of her own experience that they most closely resembled. Thus the rec-hall became "the banquet hall," the supply room became "the kitchen," the control room became "the sorcerer's tower," the tourist compartments became "the sleeping tower," Mallory's bedroom-office became "the lord's quarters," the lavatory became "the chapel," and the generator room became "the dungeon." Only two things disconcerted her: the absence of servants and the fact that Easy Money was stabled in the banquet hall. Mallory got around the first by telling her that he had given the servants a leave of absence, and she herself got around the second by declaring it to be no more than fitting for such a splendid steed to be accorded special treatment. Certainly, Mallory reflected, she was nothing if she was not co-operative.

After showing her around he wasted no time in getting down to the business on hand, and stepping into the control room, he punched out the data necessary to take the *Yore* back to 7:15 p.m. of the same day, and to re-materialize it one half mile west of its present position, as an overlap was bound to occur. There was a barely noticeable tremor as the transition took place, and simultaneously the darkness showing on the control-room telewindow transmuted to dusk.

Turning away from the jump board, he saw Rowena regarding him with large eyes from the doorway. "We're now back to a point in time that precedes the theft of the Sangraal," he told her, "and we're relocated farther down the valley. But don't let it throw you. None other than Merlin himself built the magic apparatus you see before you in this room, and you know yourself that once he makes up his mind to it, Merlin can do anything."

She blinked once, but evinced no other signs of surprise. "Yea, fair sir," she said, "I am ware of the magic of Merlin."

"However," Mallory went on, "magic such as this isn't something for a gentlewoman such as yourself to fool around with, so I must forbid you to enter this room during my absence from the castle. Also, while we're on the subject, I must also forbid you to leave the castle during my absence. Merlin would be upset no end if there were two damosels that hight Rowena gallivanting around the countryside at the same time."

She blinked again. "By my troth, fair sir," she said, "I would lever die than disobey thy two commands." And then, "Have ye ate any meat late?"

This time, Mallory blinked, "Meat?"

"It is fitting that ye should eat meat afore ye ride out."

"Oh, you mean food. I'll eat when I get back. But there's no need for you to wait." He took her into the supply room and showed her where the vacuum tins were stored. "You open them like this," he explained, pulling one out and activating the desealer. "Then, as soon as the contents cool off a little, you sit down to dinner."

"But this be not meat," she objected.

"Maybe not, but it's a good substitute, and a lot better for you." A thought struck him, and he took her into the lavatory and showed her how to operate the hot and cold-water dispenser, ascribing the setup to more of Merlin's magic. He debated on whether to explain the function and purpose of the adjacent shower, decided not to. There was a limit to all things, and an apparatus for washing one's whole body was simply too farfetched for anyone living in the sixth-century to take seriously.

Back in the rec-hall, he donned his helmet and gauntlets, reset the gauntlet timepiece, picked up his spear and encephalopathed Easy Money to his side. Mounting, he set the spear in the stirrup socket. Rowena gazed up at him, plum-blue eyes round with awe and admiration—and concern. "Wit ye well, fair sir," she said, "that Sir Launcelot, the which is thy father, is a knight of many victories, and therefore ye must take care."

Mallory grinned. "Dismay you not, fair damsel, I'll smite him from his steed before he can say 'Queen Guinevere'." He straightened his sword belt, activated the *Yore's* lock, and rode across the mirage-moat and entered the forest. The "portcullis" closed behind him.

*

Dusk had become darkness by the time he reached the highway. Approximately half an hour later he would reach the highway again.

However, the seeming paradox did not disconcert him in the least: this was far from being the first time he had backtracked himself on a job.

As "before," he spurned the shadows of the bordering oaks and beeches and encephalopathed Easy Money to keep to the center of the lane. And, as "before," no one was abroad. Probably King Pelles' wassail was already in progress, or, if not, the goodly knights and gentlewomen were still at evensong. In any event, he reached the lane that led to the castle of Carbonek without mishap.

After entering the lane, he encephalopathed Easy Money into the concealment of the shadows of the bordering trees and settled back in the saddle to wait. Rowena's placing the time of the theft at "a little while afore eight of the clock" had been a general estimate at best; hence he had allowed himself plenty of leeway and had arrived on the scene a little early. It was well that he had, for hardly a minute passed before he heard hoofbeats approaching from the south, and presently he saw a tall knight astride a resplendent steed turn into the lane. His armor gleamed in the moonlight and bespoke a quality and class that only a knight of Sir Launcelot's status would be able to afford.

Mallory watched him ride down the lane to the lion-flanked entrance and heard him announce himself as "Sir Launcelot." The portcullis was raised without delay, and the knight rode through the gateway and disappeared from view.

Mallory frowned in the darkness. Something about the incident had failed to jibe. He thought back, but he could isolate nothing that, in retrospect anyway, seemed in the least incongruous. He tried again, with the same result, and at length he concluded that the note of discord had originated in his imagination.

Again, he settled back to wait. He wasn't particularly worried about the outcome of the forthcoming encounter—the superiority of the weapons and armor should be more than enough to see him through—but just the same he wished there was some way to avoid it. There wasn't, of course. Sir Launcelot's theft of the Sangraal was already incorporated in fact, and, as a *fait accompli*, could not be obviated by a previous theft. All Mallory could do was to make his move after the *fait acccompli* in the hope that that was when he *had* made his move. A time-thief didn't have nearly as much leeway as his seeming freedom of movement might lead the uninitiated to believe. About all he could do was to play along with destiny and await his opportunities. If destiny smiled, he succeeded; if destiny frowned, he did not. However, Mallory was optimistic about his forthcoming bid for the Grail, for if it wasn't in the books for him to wrest the Cup from Sir Launcelot, the chances were he wouldn't have gotten as far as he had.

He estimated that it would take the man five minutes to enter the castle, proceed to the chamber, seize the Sangraal, return to the courtyard and come riding back to the portcullis. Seven minutes proved to be nearer the mark. In response to a hail from within the wall, several of the warders bent to the windlass, whereupon the portcullis scraped and groaned aloft, and the tall knight came riding out just as the hands of Mallory's timepiece registered 7:43 p.m.

Mallory let him pass, straining his eyes in vain for a glimpse of the Sangraal. He waited till Sir Launcelot was half a hundred yards down the highway before he encephalopathed Easy Money to follow, and he waited till a bend in the road hid the castle of Carbonek from view before encephalopathing the command to charge. At this point, Sir Launcelot became aware that he was no longer alone, and wheeled his steed around. Without an instant's hesitation, he dressed his spear and launched a counter-charge. All Mallory could think of was a twentieth-century steam locomotive bearing down upon him.

He swallowed grimly, "aventred" his own spear, and upped Easy Money's pace. Two could play at being locomotives. The approaching knight and steed loomed larger; the sound of hoofbeats crescendoed into staccato thunder. The spear pointing straight toward Mallory's breastplate had something of the aspect of a jet-propelled flagpole. Hurriedly, he got his shield into position. Maybe the man would spot the red cross, realize its significance, and slow down.

If he spotted it, he gave no sign, and only came the faster. Mallory braced himself for the forthcoming impact. However, the impact never occurred. At the last moment his antagonist directed the spearpoint at Mallory's helmet, did something that made it separate itself from the shaft to the accompaniment of a gout of incandescence and come streaking through the air like a little comet. Mallory tried to dodge, but he would have been equally as successful if he had tried to dodge a real comet. There was a deafening *clang!* in the region of his left audio-amplifier, and the whole left side of his face went numb. Just before he blacked out he saw the oncoming knight veer his steed, wheel it around, and ride off. A peal of all-too-familiar laughter drifted back over the man's shoulder.

*

"Now," said the rent-a-robogogue, "you will try again: 'A' is for 'Atom', 'B' is for 'Bomb', 'C' is for 'Conform', 'D' is for 'Dollar', 'E' is for 'Economy', and 'F' is for 'Fun'. What comes after 'F'?"

The boy Mallory squirmed in his ABC chair. "I don't know what comes next and I don't care!"

"I'll box your ears," the rent-a-robogogue threatened.

"You wouldn't dare!"

"Yes I would—I'm a physical-chastisement model, you know. Now, we'll try once more: 'A' is for 'Atom', 'B' is for 'Bomb', 'C' is for 'Conform', 'D' is for 'Dollar', 'E' is for 'Economy', and 'F' is for 'Fun'. What comes after 'F'?"

"I told you that I didn't know and that I didn't care!"

"I warned you," said the rent-a-robogogue.

"Ow!" the boy Mallory cried.

"Ow!" the man Mallory groaned, sitting up in the weeds beside the early sixth-century highway.

All was silence around him, if you discounted the stridulations of insects and the *be-ke korak-korak-korak* of frogs. A few yards away, Easy Money stood immobile in the moonlight. Mallory raised his hand to his helmet and felt the sizable dent that the spearpoint had made. Gingerly, he took the helmet off. Who in the world would have dreamed that they had jet-rifles in this day and age!

The absurdity of the thought snapped him back to full awareness. A moment later he remembered the peal of familiar laughter.

Perfidion!

The man must have wanted the Grail desperately to have come after it himself, which meant that it was probably worth much more than he had let on. But how had he known when and where to essay the lift? More specifically, how had he found out when and where to essay the lift on such short notice?

Mallory thought back. He was reasonably certain that he had made no slips of the tongue during his visit to the Perfidion Tower and during the ensuing game of golp, and he was equally certain that he had let fall no revealing references to the place-time he had so carefully pinpointed. Where, then, had he gone astray?

Suddenly, way back in his mind, Perfidion said, "By the way, Tom, I take it you're all set as regards costume, equipment and the like."

"I've got the sweetest little suit of armor you ever laid eyes on," Mallory heard himself answer.

He swore. So that was it! All Perfidion had needed to do was to make the rounds of the costumers who specialized in armor, and to shell out a few Kennedees to the one Mallory had patronized last. Then, in possession of the knowledge that Mallory was embarking into the past as Sir Galahad, all Perfidion had had to do was to consult one of the many experts he kept at his beck and call. The expert had undoubtedly told him where Sir Galahad was supposed to have found the Grail before taking it to Sarras, and, equally as important, approximately when the event was supposed to have taken place. Further questions could not have failed to elicit the additional information that Sir Launcelot had come to the chamber of the Sangraal before Sir Galahad had, and from this Perfidion had undoubtedly deduced that Sir Launcelot could very well have been a time-thief in disguise, too, and that the man, having arrived on the scene first, could very well have been responsible for the Grail's so-called return to Heaven, despite what legend said to the contrary. Certainly it had been a gamble worth taking, and obviously Perfidion had taken it.

And won the jackpot.

But that didn't mean he was going to keep the jackpot. Not by a long shot. Mallory encephalopathed Easy Money to his side and pulled himself to his feet with the help of the left stirrup and hung his helmet on the pommel. Then he picked up his spear and clambered into the saddle. "We're not beat yet, Easy Money," he said. *Giddy-ap!*

Easy Money whinnied, stamped its feet, and started back toward the *Yore*. A short while later they passed the lane that led to the castle of Carbonek. Presently Mallory heard the *clip-clop* of approaching hoofbeats, and not wanting to risk an encounter in his weakened condition, he encephalo-guided the rohorse off the highway and into the deep shadows of a big oak. There was something tantalizingly familiar about the horse and rider coming down the highway. Small wonder: the "horse" was Easy Money and the rider was himself. He was on his way to the castle of Carbonek to lift the Holy Grail.

Mallory gazed after his retreating figure disgustedly. "Sucker!" he said.

IV

Rowena nearly threw a fit when Mallory rode into the rec-hall. "Oh, fair knight, ye be sorely wounded indeed!" she cried, helping him down from his rohorse. "Certes, an ye bleed so much ye may die!"

Mallory's head was throbbing, and he saw two damosels that hight Rowena instead of only one. "I'll be all right after I lie down for a while," he said. "And don't worry about the bleeding—it's almost stopped."

He took a step in the direction of his bedroom office, staggered and would have fallen if she hadn't caught his arm. Her strength astonished him: for all the lightness of his armor, it still lent him an over-all weight of some two hundred and ten pounds; and yet the shoulder which she provided for him to lean on did not give once all the way to his bedside. She had his pauldrons, breastplate, and arm-coverings off in no time flat. His cuisses, greaves, and sollerets followed. The last he remembered was lying there in his under garments and his chain-mail vest with three faces swimming in the misted sea of his vision, each of them invested with the peculiar beauty that concern, and concern alone, can grant.

"How is mammakin's little man now?" the rent-a-mammakin asked, applying soothing sedasalve to the boy Mallory's swollen ear.

"He hit me, mammakin," the boy Mallory sobbed. "Just because I wouldn't tell him that 'G' stands for 'Geography'. I hate geography! I hate it, hate it, hate it!"

"Nasty old rent-a-robogogue! Mammakin sent him away. He was an old model that got rented out by mistake. Is mammakin's little man's ear all right now?"

The boy Mallory sat up. "I want my real—" he began.

The man Mallory sat up. "I want my real—" he began.

"I have great joy of thy swift recovery, fair sir," Rowena said.

She was perched on the edge of his bed, applying a cool and soothing ointment to his ear. On the table by the bed lay a basin of water, and on her lap lay a pink tube. He grabbed the tube, looked at the label. *Sedasalve.* He sighed with relief. "Where did you find it?" he asked.

"La! fair sir, when ye did seem no longer on live I did run both toward and forward in the castle seeking a magical salve whereby I might succor ye, whereupon I did come to a white box in the chapel wherein lay many magical tubes of diverse colors and natures whereof I did choose one and—"

Mallory was incredulous. "You chose a tube at random?" he demanded. "Good Lord, it might have contained a counteragent that could have killed me!"

"The . . . the letters thereon seemed of a magical nature, fair knight. And . . . and the color was seemly."

"Well anyway it was the right one." He looked at her. Could she read? he wondered. He was tempted to ask her, but refrained for fear of embarrassing her. "In that same white box," he said, "you will find a big bottle filled with round red pellets. Would you get it for me?"

When she returned with it, he took two of the pills, then he laid his head back on the pillow. "They'll restore the blood I lost," he explained, "but in order for them to do the job properly I've got to lie perfectly still for at least one hour."

She sat down on the edge of the bed. "Marry! the magic of Merlin is marvelous, albeit not as marvelous as the magic of Joseph of Arimathea."

"What did he do that was so marvelous?"

The plum-blue eyes were fixed full upon his face. "Ye wit naught of the tale of the white shield ye bear, fair sir? List, and I will tell ye:

"It befell after the passion of our Lord thirty-two year, that Joseph of Arimathea, the gentle knight, the which took down our Lord off the holy Cross, at that time departed from Jerusalem with a great party of his kindred with him. And so he labored till that they came to a city that hight Sarras. And at that same hour that Joseph came to Sarras there was a king that hight Evelake, that had great war against the Saracens, and in especially against one Saracen, the which was King Evelake's cousin, a rich king and a mighty, which marched nigh this land, and his name was called Tolleme la Feintes. So on a day these two met to do battle. Then Joseph, the son of Joseph of Arimathea, went to King Evelake and told him he should be discomfit and slain, but if he left his belief of the old law and believed upon the new law. And then there he showed him the right belief of the Holy Trinity, to the which he agreed unto with all his heart; and there this shield was made for King Evelake, in the name of Him that died upon the Cross. And then—"

"Hold it a minute," Mallory said. "This shield you've finally got around to mentioning—is it the same one you set out to tell me about?"

"Wit ye well, fair sir. And then through King Evelake's good belief he had the better of King Tolleme. For when Evelake was in the battle there was a cloth set afore the shield, and when he was in the greatest peril he left put away the cloth, and then his enemies saw a figure of a man on the Cross, wherethrough they all were discomfit. And so it befell that a man of King Evelake's was smitten his hand off, and bare that hand in his other hand; and Joseph called that man unto him and bade him go with good devotion touch the Cross. And as soon as that man had touched the Cross with his hand it was as whole as ever it was tofore. Then soon after there fell a great marvel, that the cross of the shield at one time vanished away that no man wist where it became. And then King Evelake was baptized, and for the most part all the people of that city. So, soon after Joseph would depart, and King Evelake would go with him whether he would or nold. And so by fortune they came into this land, that at that time was called Great Britain: and there they found a great felon paynim, that put Joseph into prison. And so—"

"A great *what?*" Mallory asked. In one sense the story was familiar to him, but what bothered him was the fact that it was familiar in another sense too—a sense he couldn't put his finger on.

"A wicked unbeliever in our Lord. And so by fortune tidings came unto a worthy man that hight Mondrames, and he assembled all his people for the great renown he had heard of Joseph; and so he came into the land of Great Britain and disinherited this felon paynim and consumed him; and therewith delivered Joseph out of prison. And after that all the people were turned to the Christian faith.

"Not long after that Joseph was laid in his deadly bed. And when King Evelake say that he made much sorrow, and said: For thy love I have left my country, and sith ye shall depart out of this world, leave me some token of yours that I may think on you. Joseph said: That will I do full gladly; now bring me your shield that I took you when ye went into battle against King Tolleme. Then Joseph bled at the nose, so that he might not by no means be staunched. And there upon that shield he made a cross of his own blood. Now may ye see a remembrance that I love you, for ye shall never see this shield but ye shall think on me, and it shall be always as fresh as it is now. And never shall man bear this shield about his neck but he shall repent it, unto the time that Galahad, the good knight, bare it; and the last of my lineage shall have it about his neck, that shall do many marvelous deeds. Now, said King Evelake, where shall I put this shield, that this worthy knight may have it? Ye shall leave it there as Nacien, the hermit, shall be put after his death; for thither shall that good knight come the fifteenth day after that he shall receive the order of knighthood: and so . . . . "

*

When Mallory awoke, Rowena's head was resting on his chest, and she was breathing the soft and even breaths of untroubled sleep. Her hair, viewed thus closely, was not as dark as he had at first believed it to be. It was brown, really, rather than dark-brown. And astonishingly lustrous. Without thinking, he rested his hand lightly upon her head. She stirred then, and sat up, rubbing her plum-blue eyes. For a moment she stared at him uncomprehendingly, then, "Prithee forgive me, fair sir," she said.

Mallory sat up, too. "Forgive you for what? Go open a couple of vacuum tins while I get into my armor—I'm going to bring this caper to a close."

"Thy . . . thy strength has returned?"

"I never felt better in my life."

In the rec-hall he said, sitting down at the table before one of the two vacuum tins she had opened, "You never did ask me what happened."

"Ye will tell me of thy own will an ye wish me to know."

Mallory took a mouthful of simulsteak, chewed and swallowed. "Your Sir Launcelot turned out to be a phony, and pulled a rabbit out of his helmet the nature of which I'd better not try to describe to you."

Eyes round as plums, she regarded him across the table. "A . . . a phony, fair sir?"

Mallory nodded. "That's a sort of felon paynim who plays golp."

"But with my own eyes I did see his armor, fair knight."

"That's right—you saw his armor. But you didn't see him. A certain character by the name of Perfidion was residing behind that hardware—not the good Sir Launcelot."

"Perfidion?"

33

Mallory grinned. "Sir Jason Perfidion—a knight errant ye wit not of. But the tournament's not over yet, and this time *I've* got the rabbit: he thinks I'm dead."

"He . . . he left ye for dead, fair sir?"

"That he did, and if that little brain-buster of his had struck just one inch to the right, I'd have been just that." He shoved his empty vacuum tin away and stood up. "Excuse me a minute—I've got to visit the sorcerer's tower again."

In the control room, he took the *Yore* back to 7:20 p.m. of the same day and re-materialized it half a mile farther down the valley. Turning, he saw that Rowena had followed him and was watching him from the doorway. "Whereabouts may I find oats that I may feed thy horse, fair knight?" she asked.

"Easy Money doesn't eat. He—" Mallory paused astonished as two of the largest tears he had ever seen coalesced in her eyes and went tumbling down her cheeks. "Oh, it's not that he's sick," he rushed on. "It's just that horses like him don't require food to keep them going. Why, Easy Money's guaranteed for . . . he'll live another thirty years."

The sun came up beyond the plum-blue horizons of her eyes. "It pleaseth me mickle to hear ye speak thus, fair knight. I . . . I have great joy of him."

Back in the rec-hall, Mallory pulled on his gauntlets, reset his timepiece, and donned his helmet. The left audio-amplifier was shot, but otherwise the piece was in good condition—aside from the dent, of course. He encephalopathed Easy Money to his side, hung his shield around his neck, and mounted. "Hand me my spear, will you, Rowena?" he asked.

She did so. "Ye be a most noble knight indeed, fair sir," she said, "for to set so little store by thine own life in the service of a damosel the which is undeserving of thy deeds. I . . . I would lever that ye forsook the Sangraal than that ye be fordone."

Her concern touched him, and he removed his helmet and leaned down and kissed her on the forehead. "Keep the home fires burning," he said; then, setting his helmet back in place, he activated the lock, rode across the mirage-moat, and set forth into the forest once again.

V

This time when he reached the crest of the ridge that separated the two valleys, Mallory took an azimuth on the towers of Carbonek, encephalo-fed the direction to Easy Money, and programmed the "animal" to proceed in as straight a course as possible.

In the east, the moon was just beginning to rise; in the west, traces of the sunset lingered blood-red just above the horizon. On the highway below, a knight sitting astride a brown rohorse and bearing a white shield with a red cross in the center was riding toward Carbonek to challenge a twenty-second century "felon paynim" in imitation Age-of-Chivalry armor. In the valley Mallory had just left behind him there were two castles named *Yore*, and soon, a third would pop into existence and yet another Mallory come riding out. Mallory grinned. It was a little bit like playing chess.

The forest which Easy Money presently entered was parklike in places, and sometimes the trees thinned out into wide, moonlit meadows. Crossing one of the meadows, Mallory saw the first star, and when at length Easy Money emerged on the highway, the heavens were decked out in typical midsummer panoply. The rohorse had followed its programming almost perfectly and had emerged at a point just south of the lane leading to the castle of Carbonek. All Mallory had to do was to encephalo-guide it farther down the highway to a point beyond the site of the forthcoming joust. While doing so, he kept well within the concealing shadows of the bordering oaks and beeches where the ground was soft and could give forth no telltale *clip-clop* of hoofbeats. His circumspection proved wise—as in one sense, of course, it already had—and when the false Sir Launcelot came riding by on his way to the castle and the chamber of the Sangraal, he was no more aware of Mallory III's presence by the roadside than he would presently be aware of Mallory II's presence in the shadows of the trees that bordered the lane.

Mallory III grinned again and brought Easy Money to a halt just beyond the next bend. "Wit ye well, Sir Jason, that thy hours be numbered," he said.

He remained seated in the saddle, feeling pretty good about the world. In no time at all, if his one-man ambuscade came off, he would be on his way back to the *Yore*, and thence to the twenty-second century and a haircut.

Selling the Sangraal without the aid of a professional time-fence like Perfidion would be difficult, of course, but it could be done, and once it was done, he, Mallory, could take his place on Get-Rich-Quick Street with the best of them, and no questions would be asked. There was, to be sure, the problem of what to do about a certain damosel that hight Rowena, but he would face that when he came to it. Maybe he could drop her off a dozen years in the future in a region far enough removed from Carbonek to ensure her safety. He would see.

At this point in his reflections he was jolted into alertness by the sound of approaching hoofbeats. A moment later he heard a second set of hoofbeats and knew that Mallory II had made his presence known. Presently both sets crescendoed into staccato thunder as the two "knights" came pounding toward each other, and not long afterward there was a clank and a clatter as Mallory II went tumbling out of his saddle and into the roadside weeds. Finally the single set of hoofbeats took over again, and Mallory III saw a horse and rider coming around the bend in the highway. He braced himself.

Before making his play, he waited till horse and rider were directly opposite him; then he encephalopathed Easy Money to charge. "Sir Launcelot" managed to get his shield up in time, but the maneuver did him no good. Mallory's spearhead struck the shield dead center, and "Sir Launcelot" went sailing out of his saddle to land with an awesome clatter flat on his back on the highway. He did not get up.

Dismounting, Mallory removed the man's helmet. It was Perfidion all right. There was a large bruise on the side of his head and he was out cold, but he was still breathing. Next, Mallory looked for the Sangraal. Perfidion had concealed it somewhere, and apparently he had done the job well. Since the armor could not have accommodated an object of that size, the hiding place had to be somewhere on the body of his horse. The horse was standing quietly beside Easy Money in the middle of the highway. It was jet-black and its fetlock-length trappings were blue, threaded with silver; otherwise, the two steeds were identical. Mallory tumbled to the truth then, went over to where the black "horse" was standing, raised its trappings, found the tiny activator button, and depressed it. The croup-hood rose up, and there in the secret compartment, wrapped in red samite, lay the cause of the mounting absentee-rate in King Arthur's court.

Always the skeptic, Mallory raised a corner of the samite in order to make certain that he was not being cheated. Instantly, a reflected ray of moonlight stabbed upward into his eyes, and for a moment he was blinded. Exorcising the thought that sneaked into his mind, he closed the croup-hood, rearranged the trappings, and returned to Perfidion's side. Dragging the armor-encumbered man over to the black rohorse and slinging him over the saddle was no easy matter, but Mallory managed; then he picked up Perfidion's helmet and spear and set the former on the pommel and wedged the latter in one of the stirrups. Finally he mounted Easy Money and, encephalopathing the black rohorse to follow, set out down the highway away from the castle of Carbonek.

Make-believe castles could fool the hadbeens, but they couldn't fool a professional. He spotted the phony towers of Perfidion's TSB rising above the trees before he had proceeded half a mile. After raising the "portcullis," he got the man down from the black rohorse, dragged him inside, and propped him against the rec-hall bar. Then he got the man's helmet and spear and laid them beside him. After considerable reflection, he went into the control room, set the time-dial for June 10, 1964, the space-dial for a busy intersection in downtown Los Angeles, and punched out H-O-T-D-O-G S-T-A-N-D on the lumillusion panel. Satisfied, he went into the generator room and short-circuited the automatic throw-out unit so that when rematerialization took place, the generator would burn up. Finding a ball of heavy-duty twine, he returned to the control room, tied one end to the master switch, and began backing out of the TSB, unwinding the twine as he went.

In the rec-hall, he paused, and grinned down at the still-unconscious Perfidion. "It's a better break than you meant to give me, Jason," he said. "And don't worry—once you explain to the authorities what you're doing in a suit of sixth-century armor and how you happened to open a giant hot-dog stand in the middle of a traffic-clogged crossroads, you'll be all right. As a matter of fact, with your knowledge of things to come, you'll probably wind up a richer man than you are now—if the smog doesn't get you first." He stepped through the lock, jerked the twine, and the "castle" vanished into thin air.

Remounting Easy Money and encephalopathing the black rohorse to follow, he started back toward the *Yore*, taking a direct route through the forest. He was halfway to his destination and had just emerged into a wide meadow when he saw the knight with the white shield riding toward him in the bright moonlight. In the center of the shield there was a vivid blood-red cross.

When the knight saw Mallory, he brought his steed to a halt. Moonlight glimmered eerily on his shield, turned his helmet to silver. His armor seemed to emit an unearthly light—a light that was at once terrifying and transcendent. The hilt of his sword was as blood-red as the cross on his shield; so was the pommel of his spear. Here was righteousness incarnate. Here in the form of an armored man on horseback was the quintessence of the Age of Chivalry—not the Age of Chivalry as exemplified by the vain and boasting nobles who had constituted nine-tenths of the knight-errantry profession and who had used the quest of the Holy Grail as an excuse to seek after mead and maidens, but the Age of Chivalry as it might have been if the ideal behind it had been shared by the many instead of by the few; the Age of Chivalry, in short, as it had come down to posterity through the pages of Malory's *Le Morte d'Arthur*.

At length the knight spoke: "I hight Sir Galahad of the Table Round."

Reluctantly, Mallory encephalopathed his two rohorses to halt, and said the only thing he had left to say: "I hight Sir Thomas of the castle *Yore*."

"By whose leave bear ye likenesses of the red arms and the white shield whereon shines the red cross the which was put there by Joseph of Arimathea whilst he lay dying in his deadly bed?"

Mallory did not answer.

There was silence. Then, "I would joust with ye," Sir Galahad said.

There it was, laid right on the line. The challenge—

The death sentence.

Nonsense! Mallory told himself. He's nothing but a nineteen-year old kid. With your rohorse and your superior weapons you can unseat him in two seconds flat, and once he's down, that glorified junk pile he's wearing will glue him to the ground so fast he won't be able to lift a finger!

Aloud, he said, "Have at me then!"

Instantly, Sir Galahad wheeled his horse around and rode to the far side of the meadow. There, he wheeled the horse around again and dressed his spear. Moonlight danced a silvery saraband on his white shield, and the blood-red cross blurred and seemed to run.

Mallory dressed his own spear. Immediately, Sir Galahad charged. *Full speed ahead, Easy Money!* Mallory encephalopathed, and the rohorse took off like a rocket.

All he had to do was to hang on tight, and the joust would be in the bag, he reassured himself. Sir Galahad's spear would break like a matchstick, while his own superior spear would penetrate Sir Galahad's shield as though the shield was made of tissue paper, as in a sense it really was when you compared the metal that constituted it to modern alloys. No matter how you looked at the situation, the kid was in for a big letdown. Mallory almost felt sorry for him.

The hoofbeats of horse and rohorse crescendoed; there was the resounding clang! of steel coming into violent contact with steel. Mallory's spear struck Sir Galahad's shield dead center—and snapped in two. Sir Galahad's spear struck Mallory's shield dead center—and Mallory sailed over Easy Money's croup and crashed to the ground.

He was stunned, both mentally and physically. Staggering to his feet, he drew his sword and raised his shield. Sir Galahad had wheeled his horse around, and now he came riding back. Several yards from Mallory, he tossed his spear aside, dismounted as lightly as though he wore no armor at all, drew his sword, and advanced. Mallory stepped forward, his confidence returning. His spear had been defective—that was it. But his sword and his shield weren't, and now that the kid had elected to give him a sporting chance, he would teach the young upstart a lesson that he would never forget.

Again, the two men came together. Down came Sir Galahad's sixth century sword; up went Mallory's twenty-second century shield. There was an ear-piercing *clang*, and the shield parted down the middle.

A KNYGHT THER WAS

Aghast, Mallory stepped back. Sir Galahad moved in, sword upraised again. Mallory raised his own sword, caught the full force of the terrific down-rushing blow on the blade. His sword was cut cleanly in two, his left pauldron was cleanly cleaved, and a great numbness afflicted his left shoulder. He went down.

He stayed down.

Sir Galahad leaned over him, unbroken sword uplifted. The cross in the center of the snow-white shield was a bright and burning red. "Ye must yield you as an overcome man, or else I may slay you."

"I yield," Mallory said.

Sir Galahad sheathed his sword. "Ye be not sorely wounded, and sithen I desire not neither of they two steeds, as belike they be as unworthy as they pieces, ye can return to thy castle unholpen."

*

Mallory blacked out for a moment, and when he came to, the shining knight was gone.

He lay there in the moonlight for some time, looking up at the stars. At length he fought his way to his feet and encephalopathed the two rohorses to his side. Mounting Easy Money, he encephalopathed it to return to the westernmost "castle of Yore" and encephalopathed the other rohorse to follow. He left his broken weapons where they lay.

What had gone out of the world during the last sixteen hundred years that had left sophisticated twenty-second century steel inferior in quality to naïve sixth-century wrought iron? What did Sir Galahad have that he, Mallory, lacked? Mallory shook his head. He did not know.

The moonlit "towers" of the *Yore* had become visible through the trees before it occurred to him that before riding away the man just might have removed the Sangraal from the black rohorse's croup. At first thought, such a possibility was too absurd to be entertained, but not on second thought. According to *Le Morte d'Arthur*, the fellowship of Sir Galahad, Sir Percivale, and Sir Bors had taken both the table of silver and the Sangraal to Sarras where, some time later, the Sangraal had been "borne up to heaven," never to be seen again. Whether they had taken the table of silver did not concern Mallory, but what did concern him was the fact that if they had taken the

Sangraal they could have done so only if it had fallen into Sir Galahad's hands this very night. Tomorrow would be too late—now was too late, in fact—provided, of course, that Mallory was destined to return with it to the twenty-second century. Here, then, was the crossroads, the real moment of truth: was he destined to succeed, or wasn't he?

Hurriedly, he encephalopathed the two rohorses to halt, dismounted, and raised the black rohorse's trappings. He was dizzy from the loss of blood, but he did not let his dizziness dissuade him from his purpose, and he had the croup-hood raised in a matter of a few seconds. He held his breath when he looked within, expelled it with relief. The Sangraal had not been disturbed.

He lifted it out of the croup-compartment, straightened its red samite covering, and cradled it in his arms. Too weak to remount Easy Money, he encephalopathed the two rohorses to follow and began walking toward the *Yore*. Rowena must have seen him coming on one of the telewindows, for she had the lock open when he arrived. Her face went white when she looked at him, and when she saw the Grail, her eyes grew even larger than plums. He went over and set it gently down on the rec-hall table, then he collapsed into a nearby chair. He had just enough presence of mind left to send her for the bottle of blood-restorer pills, and just enough strength left to swallow several of them when she brought it. Then he boarded the phantom ship that had mysteriously appeared beside him and set sail upon the soundless sea of night.

"No," said the rent-a-mammakin, "you cannot see her. She is displeased with your score in the get-rich-quick race."

"I did my best," the boy Mallory sobbed. "But when it came to stepping on all those faces, I just couldn't do it!"

The rent-a-mammakin arranged its features into a severe frown and strengthened its grip on the boy Mallory's arm. "You knew that they were only painted on the game floor to symbolize the Competitive Spirit," it said. "Why couldn't you step on them?"

The boy Mallory made a final desperate effort to gain the bedroom door which his mother had just slammed and before which the rent-a-mammakin stood, then he sank defeated to the floor. "I don't know why—I just couldn't, that's all," he sobbed. He raised his voice. "But I *will* step on them! I'll step on real faces too—just you wait and see. I'll be a bigger get-rich-quickman than my father ever dreamed of being. I'll show her!"

"I'll show her," the man Mallory murmured, "just you wait and see."

He opened his eyes. Save for himself, the bedroom-office was empty. "Rowena?"

No answer.

He raised his voice. "Rowena!"

Again, no answer.

He frowned. The door to the bedroom-office was open, and the "castle" certainly wasn't so large that his voice couldn't carry from one end of it to the other.

His shoulder throbbed faintly, but otherwise he was unaware of his wound. Rowena had bound it neatly—it was said that Age-of-Chivalry gentlewomen were quite proficient in such matters—and apparently she had once again got hold of the right counteragent.

He sat up and swung his feet to the floor. So far, so good. Tentatively, he stood up. A wave of vertigo broke over him. After it passed, he was as good as new. The blood-restorer pills had done their work well.

Nevertheless, everything was not as it should be. Something was very definitely wrong. "Rowena!" he called again.

Still no answer.

She had removed his armor and piled it neatly at the foot of the bed. He stared at the various pieces, trying desperately to think. Something had awakened him—that was it. The slamming of a door . . . or a lock.

He look a deep breath. He smelled green things. Dampness. A forest at eventide . . . .

He knew then what was wrong. The lock of the *Yore* had been opened and had been left open long enough for the evening air to permeate the interior of the TSB; long enough, in other words, to have permitted someone to ride across the imaginary drawbridge that spanned the mirage-moat. Afterward, the lock had slammed back into place of its own accord.

He hurried into the rec-hall. Easy Money stood all alone behind the tourist-bar. The black rohorse was gone.

His eyes leaped to the rec-hall table. The Sangraal was gone, too.

He groaned. The little idiot was taking it back! And after he had forbidden her to leave the "castle" too! Well no, he hadn't forbidden her exactly: he had forbidden her to leave it *during his absence*.

He walked over to the telewindow nearest the lock and scrutinized the screen. She was nowhere in sight, but night was on hand and the range of his vision, while considerably abetted by the light of the rising moon, was limited to the nearer trees.

Presently he frowned. Was it still the same night, or had he been unconscious for almost twenty-four hours?

It *couldn't* be the same night—the position of the moon disproved that. And yet he could swear that he had been unconscious for no more than a few hours.

*

Belatedly, he remembered his gauntlet timepiece, and returned to the bedroom-office. The timepiece registered 10:32. But that didn't make any sense either: the moon was still low in the sky.

He knew then that there could be but one answer, and he headed for the control room posthaste. Sure enough, the jump-board time-dial had been set for 8:00 p.m. of the same day. He looked at the space-dial. That had been set to re-materialize the *Yore* one half mile farther west.

He wiped his forehead. Good Lord, she might have sent the TSB all the way back to the Age of Reptiles! Even worse, she might have plunked it right down in the middle of WWIII!

She hadn't, though. In point of fact, she had done exactly what she had set out to do—taken the *Yore* back to a point in time from which the Sangraal could be returned to the castle of Carbonek less than an hour after it had been stolen.

Suddenly he remembered how she had watched him from the doorway of the control room each time he had reset the time and space-dials. Technologically speaking, she was little more than a child, but jump-boards were as uncomplicated as modern technology could make them, and a person needed to be but little more than a child to operate them.

Grimly, Mallory returned to his bedroom-office and got into his armor; then, ignoring the throbbing of his reawakened wound, he mounted Easy Money and set out. He had no weapons, but it could not be helped. With a little luck, he would have need of none. He was about due for a little luck, if you asked him.

He gambled that Rowena would use the same route back to the chamber of the Sangraal that they had used in leaving it—actually, she had no other choice—and he encephalo-guided Easy Money at a fast trot in the direction of the river in the hope of overtaking her before she reached the entrance to the subterranean passage. However, the hope did not materialize, and he saw no sign of her till he reached the entrance himself. Strictly speaking, he saw no sign of her then either, but he did discern several dislodged stones that could have been thrown up by the black rohorse's hoofs.

Entering the passage, he frowned. Until that moment, the incongruity of a sixth-century damosel encephalo-guiding a twenty-second century rohorse had not struck him. After a moment, though, he had to admit that the incongruity was not as glaring as it had at first seemed. "Encephalopathing" was merely a glorified term for "thinking," and Rowena, shortly after mounting Perfidion's steed, must have made the discovery that she had only to think where she wanted to go in order for the rohorse to take her there.

He had not remembered to bring a light, nor did he need one. The infrared rays of Easy Money's eye units were more than sufficient for the task on

44

hand, and overtaking the girl would have been as easy as rolling off a log—if she hadn't been riding a rohorse, too. Overtaking her wasn't of paramount importance anyway: he could confiscate the Sangraal after she returned it just as easily as he could before.

The odd part about the whole thing was that Mallory never once thought of the inevitable overlap till he saw the flicker of torchlight up ahead. An instant later he heard the sound of a woman's voice, and instinctively he encephalo-guided Easy Money into a nearby shallow cave.

*

The flickering light grew gradually brighter, and presently hoofbeats became audible. The woman's voice was loud and clear now, and Mallory made out her words above the purling of the underground stream: " . . . And then he set down the maiden, and was armed at all pieces save he lacked his spear. Then he dressed his shield, and drew out his sword, and Bors smote him so hard that it went through his shield and habergeon on the left shoulder. And through great strength he beat him down to the earth, and at the pulling of Bors' spear there he swooned. Then came Bors to the maid and said: How seemeth it to you of this knight ye be delivered at this time? Now sir, said she, I pray you lead me there as this knight had me. So shall I do gladly: and took the horse of the wounded knight, and set the gentlewoman upon him, and so brought her as she desired. Sir knight, said she, ye have better sped than ye weened, for an I had lost my maidenhead, five hundred men should have died for it. What knight was he that had you in the forest? By my faith, said she, he is my cousin. So wot I never with what engyn the fiend enchafed him, for yesterday he took me from my father privily: for I nor none of my father's men mistrusted him not, and if he had had my maidenhead he should have died for the sin, and his body shamed and dishonored for ever. Thus as . . . . "

At this point, the truth behind the sense of *deja vu* that Mallory had experienced the first time he had heard the tale hit him so hard between the eyes that he jerked back his head. When he did so, his helmet came into contact with the cave wall and scraped against the stone. The rohorse and its two riders were directly across the stream now. "*Shhh!*" Mallory I whispered.

45

A KNYGHT THER WAS

Rowena I gasped. "It were best that I thanked ye now for thy great kindness, fair knight," she said, "for anon we be no longer on live."

"Nonsense!" Mallory I said. "If this fiend of yours is anywhere in the vicinity, he's probably more afraid of us than we are of him."

"Per . . . peradventure he hath already had meat," Rowena I said hopefully. "The tale saith that an the fiend be filled he becomes aweary and besets not them the which do pass him by in peace."

"I'll keep my sword handy just in case he changes his mind," Mallory I said. "Meanwhile, get on with your autobiography—only for Pete's sake, cut it short, will you?"

"An it please, fair sir. Thus as the fair gentlewoman stood talking with Sir Bors there came twelve knights seeking after her, and anon . . . . "

For a long while after the voices faded away, Mallory IV could not move. Hearing the story the second time and, more important, hearing it from the standpoint of an observer, he had been able to identify it for what it really was—an excerpt from *Le Morte d'Arthur*. The Joseph of Arimathea bit had been an excerpt, too, he realized now, probably lifted word for word from the text. It was odd indeed that a sixth-century damosel who presumably couldn't read could be on such familiar terms with a book that would not be published for another nine hundred and forty-three years.

But not so odd if she was a twenty-second century blonde in a sixth-century damosel's clothing.

Remembering Perfidion's secretary, Mallory felt sick. No, there was no noticeable resemblance between her and the damosel that hight Rowena; but the removal of a girdle and a quarter of a pound of makeup, not to mention the application of a "lustre-rich" brown hair-dye and the insertion of a pair of plum-blue contact lenses, could very well have brought such a resemblance into being—and quite obviously had. The Past Police were noted for their impersonations, and most of them had eidetic memories.

Come on, Easy Money, Mallory encephalopathed. *You and I have got a little score to settle.*

*

When he entered the chamber of the Sangraal, Rowena IV was arranging the red samite cover around the Grail. She jumped when she saw him. "Marry! fair sir, ye did startle me. Methinketh ye be asleep in thy castle."

"Knock it off," Mallory said. "The masquerade's over."

She regarded him with round uncomprehending eyes. He got the impression that she had been crying. "The . . . the masquerade, fair knight?"

"That's right . . . the masquerade. You're no more the damosel Rowena than I'm the knight Sir Galahad."

She lowered her eyes to his breastplate. "I . . . I wot well ye be not Sir Galahad, fair sir. It . . . it happed that aforetime I did see Sir Galahad with my own eyes, and when ye did unlace thy unberere and I did see thy face, I knew ye could not be him of which ye spake." Abruptly she raised her head and looked at him defiantly. "But I knew from thy eyes that ye be most noble, fair sir, and therefore an ye did pretend to be him the which ye were not, ye did so for noble cause, and it were not for me to question."

"I said knock it off," Mallory said, but with considerable less conviction. "I'm onto you—don't you see? You're a time-fink."

"A . . . a time fink? I wot not what—"

"An agent of the Past Police. One of those do-gooders who run around history replacing stolen goods and turning in hard-working people like myself. You gave yourself away when you lifted that Sir Bors bit straight out of *Le Morte d'Arthur* and—"

"But I did say ye sooth, fair sir. Sir Bors did verily succor my maidenhead. I wot not how there can be two of ye and two of me and four hackneys when afore there were but two, and I wot not how by touching the magic board in thy castle in a certain fashion that I could make the hour earlier and I wot not how the magic steed I did bestride brought me hither—I wot not none of these matters, fair sir. I wot only that the magic of thy castle is marvelous indeed."

For a while, Mallory didn't say anything. He couldn't. In the plum-blue eyes fixed full upon his face, truth shone, and that same truth had invested her every word. The damosel Rowena, despite all evidence to the contrary and despite the glaring paradox the admission gave rise to, was not a phony, never had been a phony, and never would be a phony. She was, as a matter of fact—with the exception of Sir Galahad—the only completely honest person he had known in all his life.

"Tell me," he said, at length, "weren't you afraid to come back through that passage alone? Weren't you afraid the fiend would get you?"

"La! fair sir—I had great fear. But it were not fitting that I bethought me of myself at such a time." She paused. Then, "What might be thy true name, sir knight?"

"Mallory," Mallory said. "Thomas Mallory."

"I have great joy of thy acquaintance, Sir Thomas."

Mallory only half heard her. He was looking at the samite-covered Sangraal. No more obstacles stood between him and his quest, and time was a-wasting. He started to take a step in the direction of the silver table.

His foot did not leave the floor.

*

He was acutely aware of Rowena's eyes. As a matter of fact, he could almost feel them upon his face. It wasn't that they were any different than they had been before: it was just that he was suddenly and painfully cognizant of the trust and the admiration that shone in them. Despite himself, he had the feeling that he was standing in bright and blinding sunlight.

Again, he started to take a step in the direction of the silver table. Again, his foot did not leave the floor.

It wasn't so much the fact that she didn't believe he would take the Sangraal that bothered him: it was the fact that she couldn't conceive of him taking it. She could be convinced that black was white, perhaps, and that white was black, and that fiends hung out in empty caves and castles; but she could never be convinced that a "knight" of the qualities she imputed to Mallory could perform a dishonorable act.

And there it was, laid right on the line. For all the good the Grail was going to do Mallory, it might just as well have been at the bottom of the Mindanao Deep.

He sighed. His gamble hadn't paid off any more than Perfidion's had. The real Sir Galahad was the one who had inherited the Grail after all—not the false one. The false one grinned ruefully. "Well," he told the damosel

Rowena, "it's been nice knowing you." He swallowed; for some reason his throat felt tight. "I . . . I imagine you'll be all right now."

To his amazement she broke into tears. "Oh, Sir Thomas!" she cried. "In my great haste to return the Sangraal to the chamber and to right the grievous wrong committed by the untrue knight Sir Jason, I did bewray my trust again. For when I espied ye and me and Easy Money in the passage I did suffer a great discomfit, and it so happed that when my steed did enter into a cave that the Sangraal came free from my hands and . . . and—"

Mallory was staring at her. "You *dropped* it?"

Stepping over to the silver table, she lifted a corner of the red samite. The dent was not a deep one, but just the same you didn't have to look twice to see it. "I . . . I nyst not what to do," she said.

Suddenly Mallory remembered the first sound he had heard in the passage when he and Rowena were leaving the castle of Carbonek. "Well how do you like that!" he said. He grinned. "I take it that this puts your hands in jeopardy all over again—right?"

"Yea, Sir Thomas, but I would lever die than beseech thee again to—"

"Which," Mallory continued happily, "makes it out of the question for a knight such as myself to leave you behind." He took her arm. "Come on," he said. "I don't know how I'm going to fit a sixth-century damosel into twenty-second century society, but believe me, I'm going to try!"

"And . . . and will ye take Easy Money to this land whereof ye speak, Sir Thomas?"

"Sir Thomas" grinned. "Wit ye well," he said, "and his buddy, too. Come on."

*

In the *Yore*, he tossed his helmet and gauntlets into a corner of the rec-hall and proceeded straight to the control room. There, with Rowena standing at his elbow, he set the time-dial for June 21, 2178 and the space-dial for the Kansas City Time-Tourist Port. Lord, it would be good to get home again and get a haircut! "Here goes," he told Rowena, and threw the switch.

There was a faint tremor. "Brace yourself, Rowena," he said, and took her over to the control-room telewindow.

Together, they gazed upon the screen. Mallory gasped. The vista of spiral suburban dwellings which he had been expecting was not in the offing. In its stead was a green, tree-stippled countryside. In the distance, a castle was clearly discernible.

He stared at it. It wasn't a sixth-century job like Carbonek—it was much more modern. But it was still a castle. Obviously, the jump-board had malfunctioned and thrown the *Yore* only a little ways into the future, the while leaving it in pretty much the same locale.

He returned to the jump-board to find out. Just as he reached it, its lights flickered and went out. The time and space-dials, however, remained illumined long enough for him to see when and where the TSB had re-materialized. The year was 1428 A.D.; the locale, Warwickshire.

Mallory made tracks for the generator room. The generator was smoking, and the room reeked with the stench of shorted wires.

He swore. Perfidion!

So that was why the man had broken with tradition and invited a common time-thief to a game of golp!

If he had been anyone but Perfidion he would have gimmicked the controls of the *Yore* so that Mallory would have wound up directly in the fifteenth century sans sojourn in the sixth. But being Perfidion, he had wanted Mallory to know how completely he was being outsmarted. The chances were, though, that if the man had anticipated the near-coincidence of the two visits to the chamber of the Sangraal he would have seen to it that Mallory had never gotten a chance to use his Sir Galahad suit.

Returning to the control room, Mallory saw that the lumillusion panel had been pre-programmed to materialize the *Yore* as a fifteenth-century English castle. Apparently it had been in the books all along for him to become a fifteenth-century knight, just as it had been in the books all along for Perfidion to become the proprietor of a misplaced hot-dog stand.

Mallory laughed. He had gotten the best of the bargain after all. At least there was no smog in the fifteenth century.

Who was he supposed to be? he wondered. Had his name gone down in history by any chance?

Abruptly he gasped. Was *he* the Sir Thomas Malory with estates in Northamphshire and Warwickshire? Was *he* the Sir Thomas Malory who had compiled and translated and written *Le Morte d'Arthur*? Almost nothing about the man's life was known, and probably the little that was known had been assumed. He *could* have popped up from nowhere, made his fortune through foreknowledge, and been knighted. He *could* have been a reformed time-thief stranded in the fifteenth century.

But if he, Mallory, was Malory, how in the world was he going to get five hundred chapters of semi-historical data together and pass them off as *Le Morte d'Arthur*?

Suddenly he understood everything.

*

Going over to where Rowena was still standing in front of the telewindow, he said, "I'll bet you know no end of stories about the doings of the knights of the Table Round."

"La! Sir Thomas. Ever I saw day of my life I have heard naught else in the court of my father."

"Tell me," Mallory said, "how did this Round Table business begin? Or, better yet, how did the Grail business begin? We can take up the Round Table business later on."

She thought for a moment. Then, "List, fair sir, and I will say ye: At the vigil of Pentecost, when all the fellowship of the Round Table were come unto Camelot and there heard their service, and the tables were set ready to the meat, right so entered into the hall a full fair gentlewoman on horseback, that had ridden full fast, for her horse was all besweated. Then she there alit, and came before the king and saluted him; and he said: Damosel, God thee bless. Sir, said she, for God's sake say me where Sir Launcelot is. Yonder ye may see him, said the king. Then she went unto Launcelot and said: Sir Launcelot, I salute you on King Pelles' behalf, and I require you to come on with me hereby into a forest. Then Sir Launcelot asked her with whom she dwelled. I dwell, said she, with King Pelles. What will ye with me? said Launcelot. Ye shall know, said she, when ye—"

A KNYGHT THER WAS

"That'll do for now," Mallory interrupted. "We'll come back to it as soon as I get stocked up on paper and ink. Scheherazade," he added.

"Scheherazade, Sir Thomas? I wot not—"

He leaned down and kissed her. "There's no need for you to wot," he said. Probably, he reflected, he would have to do a certain amount of research in order to record the happenings that had ensued his and Rowena's departure, and undoubtedly said research would result ironically in the recording of the true visits of Sirs Galahad and Launcelot to the chamber of the Sangraal—the "time-slots" on which he and Perfidion had gambled and lost their shirts. The main body of the work, however, had been deposited virtually on his lap, and its style and flavor had been arbitrarily determined. Moreover, contrary to what history would later maintain, the job would not be done in prison, but right here in the "castle of Yore" with Rowena sitting—and dictating—beside him. As for the impossibility of giving a sixth-century damosel as his major source, that could be avoided—as in one sense it already had been—my making frequent allusions to imaginary French sources. And as for the main obstacle to the endeavor—his twenty-second century cynicism—that had been obviated during his encounter with Sir Galahad.

The book wouldn't be published till 1485, but just the same, he was keen to get started on it. Writing it should be fun. Which reminded him: "I know we haven't known each other very long in one sense, Rowena," he said, "but in another, we've known each other for almost nine hundred years. Will you marry me?"

She blinked once. Then her plum-blue eyes showed how truly blue they could become and she threw her arms around his gorget. "Wit ye well, Sir Thomas," said she, "that there is nothing in the world but I would lever do than be thy bride!"

Thus did the prose epic known
successively as "La Mort d'Arthur,"
THE MOST ANCIENT
AND FAMOUS HISTORY OF THE
RENOWNED PRINCE ARTHUR,
KING OF BRITAINE,

ROBERT F. YOUNG

AS ALSO, ALL THE NOBLE ACTS,
AND HEROICKE DEEDS
OF HIS VALIANT KNIGHTS
OF THE ROUND TABLE,
and "Le Morte d'Arthur"
come to be recorded.